ANGER'S WAY OUT

GRADES 3-6

How Sam Learned to Express Her Angry Feelings in a Healthy Way

By Karen Biron-Dekel

Illustrated by Joseph Underdue

youth light inc.

© 2011 by YouthLight, Inc. | Chapin, SC 29036

Cover Design by: Amy Rule
Layout and Design by Melody Taylor
Project Editing by Susan Bowman

Library of Congress Control Number
2011920217

ISBN
978-159850-103-2

10 9 8 7 6 5 4 3 2 1
Printed in the United States

Acknowledgements

With special thanks to Krystina Anne Groce for her spontaneous creativity, which resulted in the long-awaited title of this book. My thanks, as well, to Jill Goldstein, for her unlimited resourcefulness and insightful suggestions. I am ever so grateful to Grace Pariti, for bringing this publisher to my attention and to Moshe, for his loving support throughout this literary journey. And, finally, to Lauren, who provided the spark and inspiration for this story and without whom this book might never have evolved.

This book would not be complete without a special acknowledgement of my son, Michael, and all of our children in the Armed Forces, whose daily sacrifice and heroism keep our country safe and allow us the freedom to enjoy and teach the lessons of this book. My love and prayers are always with you.

To my children,
Lauren and Michael,
with love and pride.

TABLE OF CONTENTS

Sam groaned in her bed. Why did it seem like Mom always woke her at the best part of her dream? She loved reliving that moment...the crowd cheering wildly, her parents' proud faces in the stands, her teammates rushing up and jumping all over her!

"Maybe they're going to tell me where we're going on our road trip this summer," Sam hoped as she got dressed.

"Family adventures," her mom liked to call them. They promised to talk about it after she got her report card. "Thank the Lord I got straight A's," Sam thought to herself, as she pranced down the stairs.

Mom and Dad looked very serious. "Hi, Sam," they said. "There's something we need to talk to you about."

"Uh oh... What did I do now?" Sam wondered.

As she joined them at the table, Mom asked if she had noticed that there had been a lot of arguing lately. "Sure," Sam said, "But I thought all parents fight sometimes." "That's true," said her Mom, "But sometimes they have problems that they just can't fix."

Sam was starting to feel very nervous inside.

"Are you saying what I think you're saying?"

The painful look in Mom's eyes answered before her words could.

"Sam, Dad and I are getting a divorce."

Dad added, "Mom and I want you to understand that even though we may have stopped loving each other, we will never stop loving you." "I know *that*," she replied, forcing a smile.

Sam really needed to be alone. She gave them each a hug and said, "I'm not very hungry right now. I think I'll go upstairs and work on my project."

Sam laid in her bed for hours.
She felt numb.
Her whole world was falling apart, and
there was nothing, absolutely nothing,
that she could do about it.

After a long while, a lot of different feelings began to stir around inside her.

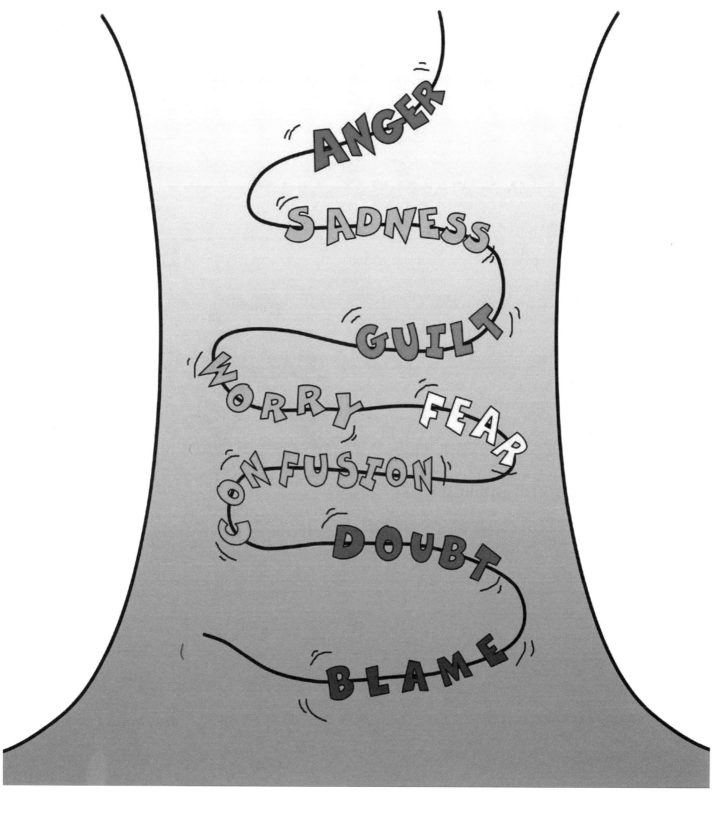

At first, Sadness welled up...

...and tears came spilling out.

Then Fear and Worry jumped out together...

...and made her heart pound really fast.

Pretty soon, there was only one feeling left down inside Sam.
His name was Anger.

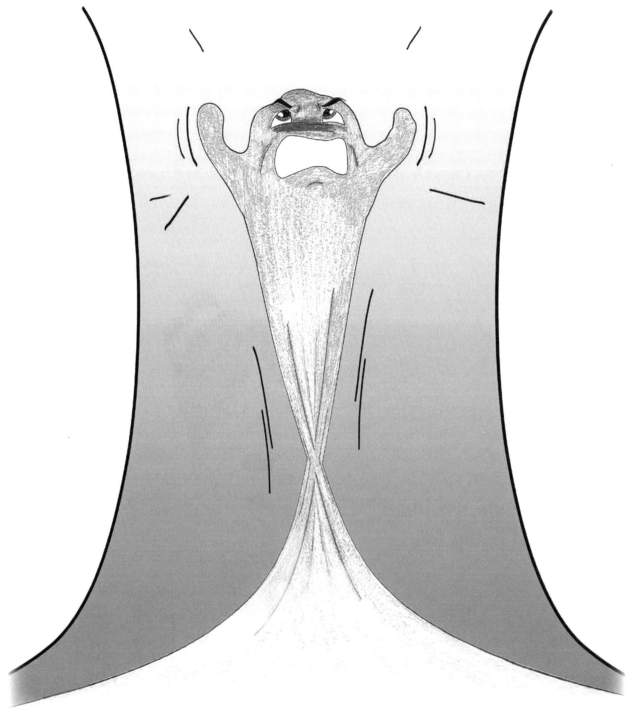

No matter how many times he tried to push his way up,
Sam always found a way to hold Anger down.

Sam remembered the time when her Dad got so mad that he almost punched a hole right through the wall. She'd never forget how scared she was.

BAM!

Sam never wanted her Anger to take control of her like that.
She feared all sorts of terrible things would happen to her or to someone she loved if she couldn't control her Anger...so she just ignored him.

"Hey, Sam!" he would call. "Let me out!"
"No way!"

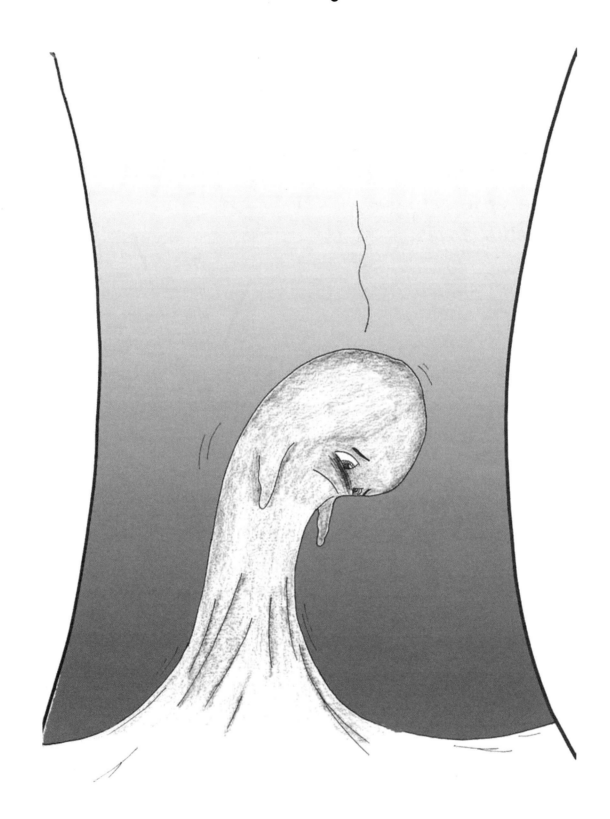

Poor Anger would sink back down feeling sad and lonely.

Whenever new feelings grew inside Sam, Anger felt comforted that he was not alone. But as soon as those feelings got big enough, they called up to Sam and she always let them out.

Anger couldn't believe it! "What about me?" he would beg.
But Sam just pretended that she didn't hear him.
Pretty soon, Anger started to get really mad.

"How dare you let up all your other feelings and leave me behind!
This is just not fair. You're going to be sorry for this, missy!"

Anger began to roll around in Sam's stomach with such force, that she developed bad stomach aches. Some days they were so bad that she couldn't go to school.

Still, Sam did not pay any attention to him.

Anger needed a plan. He thought about all the possible exit routes. The most logical seemed to be the mouth. He could simply hide out on top of Sam's voice box and be carried out on a wave of laughter.

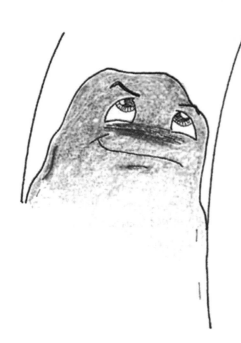

Anger was so pleased with himself. He couldn't wait for his chance to escape.

But Sam felt Anger rising in her throat. She didn't feel much like laughing at all. In fact, her face became very tense and she barely smiled anymore, but she didn't care, because it kept Anger down.

|

Anger was getting desperate. He tried slipping through Sam's air passages. He figured she'd never notice him there. But, once again, Sam outsmarted him. She developed asthma. Now, her bronchial tubes were squeezed so tightly together, that it was very hard for her to breathe.

Her coughing spells were so bad when she ran that she had to quit the soccer team. It was well worth it, though, because it kept Anger down.

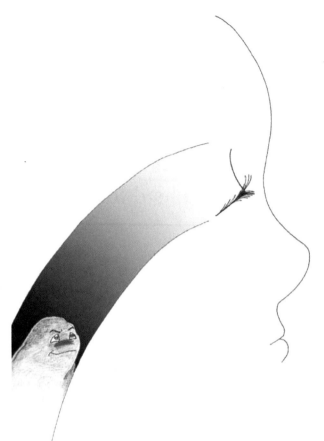

Sam even developed a tic in her eye to prevent Anger from escaping when her eyelids were opened. As soon as she felt him coming through, the blinking started up and she blinked him back down.

It's true, the tic was embarrassing, but at least it kept Anger down.

Well, Anger got angrier. And the angrier Anger got, the bigger he got.

It was becoming a lot of pressure for Sam to keep Anger down all the time.

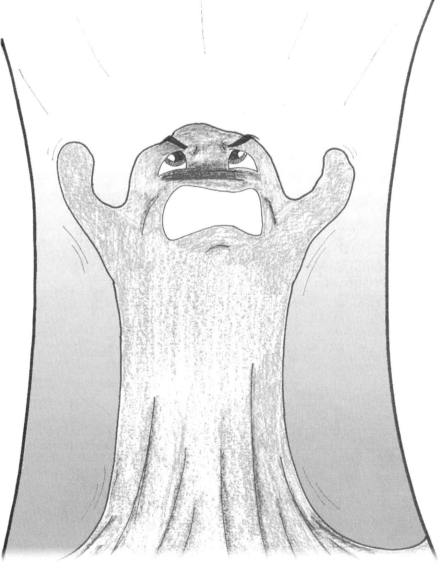

|

To make matters worse, her Mom met a new man, named Martin. She spent so much time with him that Sam was afraid Mom would start loving Martin more than she loved her!

Sam began to have trouble paying attention in school. She wasn't getting along with her friends as well as she used to, either. Lately, everyone seemed to be getting on her nerves. Sam had to face it. Anger was starting to have a really bad effect on her life.

"There's got to be a way to bury this Anger once and for all," Sam grumbled. She wracked her brain for the perfect plan.

Finally it came to her!

"If I stuff myself with enough food, I just might be able to crush Anger forever," she reasoned.

And so she ate...and ate...and ate.

The more Anger tried to push up, the more she ate. Sam gained so much weight that kids started to make fun of her. "A small price to pay to keep Anger down", she reminded herself as she walked past the snickering and finger pointing.

But as you might have guessed, Anger was not going to be kept down.

Anger decided to try the direct approach. Curling into a tight ball, he shot straight into Sam's head, hoping to burst right through the top.

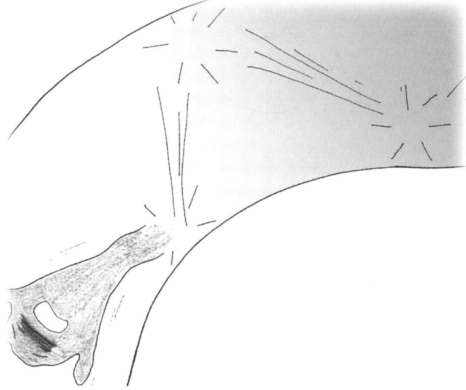

But, instead, he just bounced back down, banging around helplessly.

This caused Sam some of the worst headaches she ever had, but she would deal with them, because it kept Anger down.

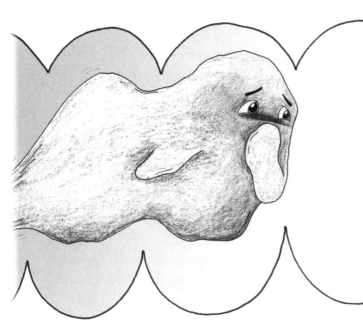

As a last resort, Anger considered the least appealing exit...sneaking through Sam's intestines.

He took a deep breath as he entered.
He hoped this would be quick.

Sam felt a painful sensation in the lower part of her belly. She guessed what Anger was up to.

Her intestinal muscles clenched automatically, blocking Anger's escape.

Unfortunately, this blockage also backed up all the food Sam was digesting, causing her very bad cramps.

Thankfully, Anger did not choose this path again.

One day Anger was rolling around inside Sam, feeling totally frustrated and helpless, when he bumped into a young lad he'd never seen before.

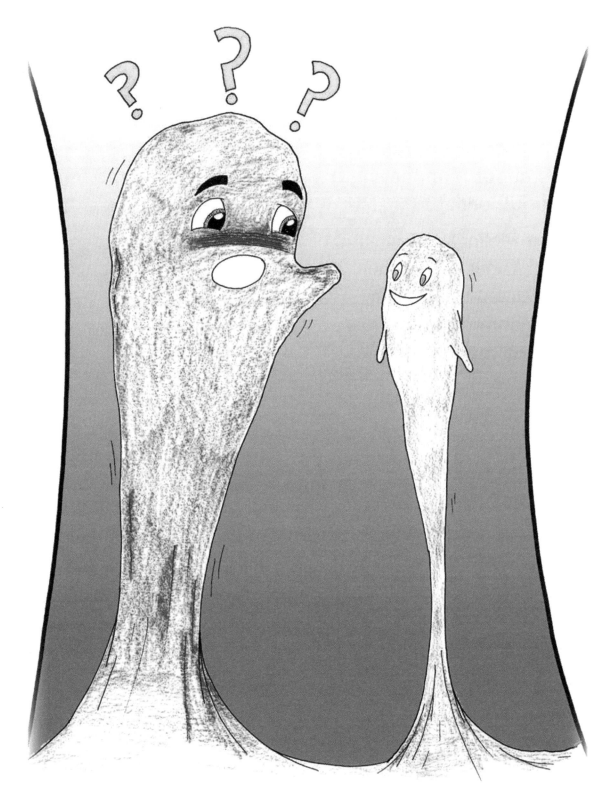

"Who are you?" Anger asked. "I'm Anger," replied the little guy. "But how can you be Anger when I'm Anger?" Anger wanted to know.

"It's simple," said the smaller one. "We're both part of the same family.

Your anger is about Mom wanting a divorce. My anger is about Dad leaving.

Come, I'll introduce you to the newest member of our family. His anger is about Mom having a boyfriend."

All the angry feelings sat around and got to know each other. Anger realized how much they had in common, yet how different they were.

"I think the problem is that Sam doesn't know we are separate feelings. She thinks anger is one big feeling.

We all feel the same to her, so she thinks that we all have to come out together. That feels too big and powerful to her.

She's afraid it would hurt too much if we all came charging through."

"Maybe we need to separate and let her feel us one at a time."

"Let's try it!" the others agreed.

|

All the anger inside of Sam formed a single line.
Sam's Anger about Mom wanting a divorce came forward first.
He waited until Sam was talking to her Mom and then
called up to her.

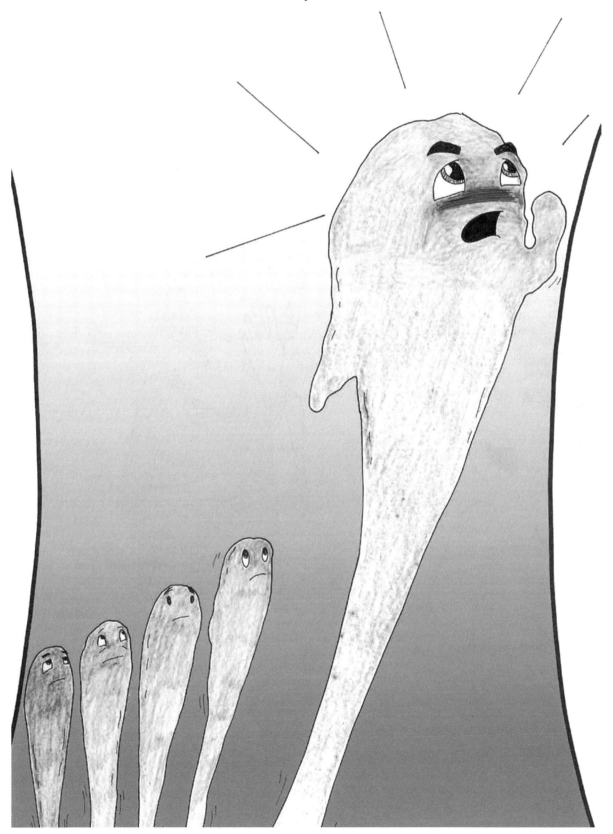

Now that Sam only felt Anger about the divorce, she was able to let him out because he did not seem as threatening to her. "It makes me so angry that you broke up our family. How could you do this to us? Don't you know that nobody wanted this divorce but you? How could you be so selfish?" Sam felt the Anger streaming out of her.

The more Sam let her Anger out, the better she started to feel.
And the funny thing was, her Mom didn't get mad at her, or leave her,
like Sam feared she would. She actually seemed to understand.
Sam felt sooo relieved.

Mom even introduced her to a really kind and caring person named
Dr. Foster, who helped Sam understand the rest of her angry feelings.
Dr. Foster played games with Sam and gave her suggestions on how
to get the rest of her anger out, in healthy ways. From then on,
whenever Sam started feeling angry, she would go for a run or
write her feelings down in a diary. If Anger was still stuck,
she would talk to her mom about them.

It took a long time to get all her anger out, but as she did, wonderful things started to happen. Her face began to relax, the tics disappeared, her beautiful smile returned, and so did her friends. She no longer suffered from stomach aches or headaches. Sam lost all the weight she had gained. Even her asthma improved.

|

And now, whenever any feelings start calling to come out,
Sam just reaches down inside herself, and lets them go.

ANGER'S WAY OUT

STORY REVIEW

Objective: Students will demonstrate an understanding of the concepts illustrated in the book, "Anger's Way Out."

Materials: "Anger's Way Out" by Karen Biron-Dekel, "Anger's Way Out" Worksheets.

Procedures:

1. Either read the book aloud or have the students read their own copy, depending on age appropriateness.

2. Distribute the worksheets and have the students complete.

3. Allow them to go back to the book to find the answers to questions with which they were having difficulty.

4. Review the worksheets as a class.

5. Pair the students and have them discuss their favorite part of the book or a part to which they could particularly relate.

6. Ask for volunteers to share their responses back in the larger group.

Directions: Write out your responses and share with the class.

What do you notice about the girl on the cover of the book?

_____

_____

How do you think she's feeling? Have you ever felt this way? When?

_____

_____

What change is going on in Samantha's life?

_____

_____

What do Sam's parents want her to understand?

_____

_____

Circle the feelings that begin to stir inside Sam:

Joy   Blame   Guilt   Happiness   Fear   Confidence

Worry   Doubt   Confusion   Peace   Anger   Sadness

Draw a star ⭐ on the only feeling that didn't "push"
its way out of Sam!

Who was preventing Anger from being pushed out?

_____

Directions: Draw a line through the false answer in each column below:

Ways Anger tried to get out	What happens to Sam's body?
Rolled around in Sam's stomach	Bad stomach aches
Hid on top of Sam's voice box	She turned red
Slid through Sam's air passages	Asthma
Added pressure	Tics

What made matters worse for Sam?

_____

_____

What was she afraid would happen?

_____

_____

What do you think Sam should have said to her mother?

_____

_____

Directions: Complete the questions below:

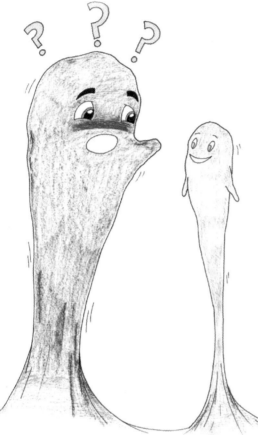

Who did Anger bump into one day?

_____

_____

_____

What doesn't Sam know about these "angry feelings"?

_____

_____

_____

What plan do the "angry feelings" make to leave Sam's body?

_____

_____

Did their plan work?

_____

_____

How did Sam feel once she let her angry feelings out?

_____

_____

What did Sam learn to do whenever any feelings start to come out?

_____

_____

_____

What did you learn from Sam's experience?

_____

_____

_____

What will you be sure to do the next time you realize that you are holding feelings in?

_____

_____

Objective: Students will identify a variety of feelings, examine the differences in how we feel inside and how we act on the outside, and learn why it is important to communicate feelings effectively.

Materials: "Anger's Way Out" by Karen Biron-Dekel, "My Inside and Outside Feelings" Handout, pen, marker, whiteboard or flip chart.

Procedure:

1. Direct the students to look at the Feelings welling up inside Sam, on page 7, of "Anger's Way Out."

2. Ask the class to think of other feelings and write down as many as they can.

3. Make 2 columns on the board – "Pleasant Feelings" and "Unpleasant Feelings."

4. Explain that all feelings are normal. No feelings are "bad," but some feelings make you feel good inside while others don't feel good.

5. Ask for volunteers to come to the front, one at a time, to write an emotion in the appropriate column.

6. When the lists are complete, have the students pick one feeling from each column, that they have experienced, write them on the "My Inside and Outside Feelings worksheet," and write how it made them feel inside and how they acted on the outside.

7. Divide the class into groups of four and instruct the students to take turns describing or miming how they acted on the outside, for each of the two feelings, without stating the actual feeling. The others should try to guess the feelings, with each student getting one guess for each feeling.

8. Return to the larger group and share how easy it was to tell how a person was feeling by the way they acted and whether if was easier to guess the pleasant feeling or the unpleasant feeling.

9. Have the students write a statement about what they learned from this exercise and why it is important to communicate their inner feelings clearly.

My Inside and Outside Feelings

Directions: Using the grid below, think of a time when you experienced a pleasant feeling and an unpleasant feeling.

Pleasant Feeling	How I Felt Inside	How I Acted on the Outside

Unpleasant Feeling	How I Felt Inside	How I Acted on the Outside

LESSON 2: DEALING WITH LOSS

Objective: Students will explore feelings that can emerge by unwanted change. Students will understand that change involves loss. Students will become familiar with the feelings that are typically experienced during loss.

Materials: "Anger's Way Out" by Karen Biron-Dekel, paper and markers, crayons, etc., and a copy of the "My Personal Change" flow chart.

Procedure:

1. Read aloud the first six pages of "Anger's Way Out."

2. Ask the students what changed in Sam's life that made her upset.

3. Explain that sometimes things happen that we can't control. When things change in our lives, we experience a loss of the way things used to be.

4. Ask the students to think of a time when they felt sad or to imagine a situation that would make them sad. Give examples if necessary, i.e. loss of a pet, family member, move to another home, a fight resulting in the end of a friendship.

5. Have the students write the situation on the following flow chart.

6. On the next level of the flow chart, ask the students to write 3 ways in which life was different because of the situation.

7. Explain that when an unwanted change happens in our lives, it is normal to experience many different feelings, some of the most common being Shock, Numbness, Sadness, Anger, Fear, Guilt, Worry and Loneliness. Write these feelings on the board. Explain that it is normal to feel these feelings for weeks or even months, depending on how upsetting the situation was.

8. Now have the students write, on the third level of the flow chart, how each change made them feel (or would make them feel in the imagined situation).

9. Ask what made them feel better (or what they think would make them feel better). Give suggestions, if necessary, i.e., talking about their feelings, accepting the reality of the change, looking at the positive aspects of the change, etc.

My Personal Change Flow Chart

Situation

Change #1		Change #2		Change #3

Feeling #1		Feeling #2		Feeling #3

Objective: Students will expand their vocabulary of anger words and understand the importance of expressing anger in a healthy way.

Materials: "Anger's Way Out" by Karen Biron-Dekel, small balloon, whiteboard, marker, paper and pen.

Preparation: Partially blow up the balloon, leaving room for another large breath of air. Draw a face on the balloon.

Procedure:

1. Ask the students to think of different words that describe anger. List responses on the board.

2. Read aloud pages 7-15 of "Anger's Way Out." Discuss the fact that people handle their anger in different ways. How did Sam handle her anger?

3. Break students into pairs and ask them to decide if it is better to hold anger in or let it out.

4. Return to the larger group and have them share their opinions.

5. Hold up the balloon and say, "This balloon represents you. The air I blow into it represents your angry feelings." Blow the balloon to the max and say, "Now you look ready to explode. How can we get you to return to normal?" (They should respond, "Release some anger, let your angry feelings out", etc.)

6. Follow their command and let just enough air out for the balloon to return to its original size and say, "That's correct, when you release your anger, you return to your normal state."

7. Now ask, "What will happen if I keep blowing more angry feelings in, without releasing any?" When they answer, "The balloon will pop, or explode," you respond, "That is exactly what happens to us if we hold in our anger, and let it keep building...we feel like exploding."

8. Ask the class, "Can you think of an example of how a person might act when their anger explodes? Write the examples on the board. (i.e., punch someone, scream and curse, hurt themselves or an animal, damage something, etc.)

9. On a piece of paper, have them finish the sentence, "It is important to let my anger out in a healthy way because..."

SOCCER

OPTIONAL ACTIVITIES ON ANGER PATTERNS

• After reading "Anger's Way Out," refer to page 32, in which Sam lets out her anger toward her mom.

• Explain that anger is normal and we all get angry sometimes. Ask the students to raise their hands if they ever get angry at anyone.

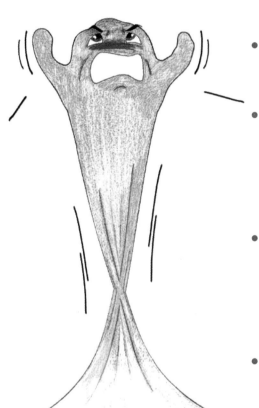

• Distribute the "Anger Patterns" worksheets and have students complete.

• Ask students if they learned anything from their charts and graphs that surprised them.

• Direct the students to pick a situation in which they had a verbal or physical fight with someone and draw a cartoon strip depicting it.

• When they are finished, have them draw another strip of the same scenario, only this time, with an ending in which they do not get as angry, or do not get angry at all.

• Break the students into pairs and have them exchange cartoon strips. The other student will create a third version, which does not involve fighting or arguing.

• Return to the larger group and share some of the alternative endings, adding some of your own, if appropriate.

• Instruct the students to try and remember some of these suggestions for resolving problems without fighting the next time they start to get angry.

Anger Patterns

ADULTS	SIBLINGS	FRIENDS	BULLIES

1. Think of the people in your life that you fight with (verbally or physically). What is their relation to you?

2. Write their initials in a circle in the appropriate box above.

3. How angry do you usually get with each person? Color the circle with their initials:
   Orange – if you get Angry
   Purple – if you get Very Angry
   Red – if you get Furious

4. How often do you fight with each person? Show on the bar graph below.
   Initials

   -
   -
   -
   -
   -
   -
   -
   -

   | | | | |
   | Daily | At least once a week | Every once in a while | Hardly ever |

5. How long do the fights last? Show on the bar graph below.

-
-
-
-
-
-
-
-
- _____|_____|_____|_____|

     Daily   At least once a week   Every once in a while   Hardly ever

ANGER CAUSES AND EFFECTS

- Read "Anger's Way Out" aloud to the class.

- Ask the students what caused Sam to be angry.

- Distribute the worksheets and tell students to make a list of reasons that they get angry.

- Discuss reasons as a group and write general reasons on the board (i.e., feeling frustrated, losing control, getting hurt, being left out, being teased, getting embarrassed, being lied to, not feeling good enough, getting bad grades, being "bossed," etc.).

- Explain that when we get angry our bodies and minds react to the emotion.

- Direct the students to complete the bottom half of the worksheet.

- Have the students share their responses and write them on the board. Add any reactions they may have missed i.e., Physical – fast heart beat, sweating, tight muscles, tension on face, red face and neck, shaking, clenched jaw, fists, rapid breathing, headaches, stomach aches, cramps, tics. Emotional – yelling, cursing, throwing things, irritability, problems focusing, poor memory, poor grades, overeating.

- Ask the students what effects Anger had on Sam. Have volunteers come to the board and circle the words from your list.

WHAT CAUSES MY  **ANGER**

_____

_____

_____

_____

_____

_____

HOW MY **ANGER** AFFECTS ME

Physically   Emotionally

_____   _____

_____   _____

_____   _____

_____   _____

_____   _____

_____   _____

NEGATIVE AND POSITIVE WAYS TO HANDLE ANGER

• Discuss with the class positive ways to deal with anger.

(Examples of positive ways to deal with anger: Count to 10, talk to someone about your feelings, write feelings down in a diary or journal, exercise, bike, run/walk, dance, use a punching bag, sports, yoga, distract yourself with an activity, (i.e., art, music, poetry, reading, video games, TV, etc.)

(Examples of negative ways to deal with anger: Hitting, pushing, choking, or biting someone, throwing things, cursing, screaming, hurting yourself or animals, destroying property, etc.)

• Summarize to the group that students should find the way(s) to release anger that work(s) best for them. They can do anything that works for them as long as it's not hurtful to themselves, others, or animals; it's not destructive, and won't make the situation worse.

• Students should now fill out the questionnaire on "How I Deal with Angry Feelings."

• Ask the students what new ways they learned from this exercise that they will try the next time they get angry.

How I Deal with Angry Feelings

Describe a situation that made you angry.

_____

_____

_____

_____

_____

How did you handle it?

_____

_____

_____

_____

_____

Do you think that was the best way to handle it?

_____

_____

_____

_____

_____

Why or why not?

_____

_____

_____

_____

_____

What other ways could you have handled it?

_____

_____

_____

_____

_____

Directions: Write on the lines below some negative and positive ways to handle anger.

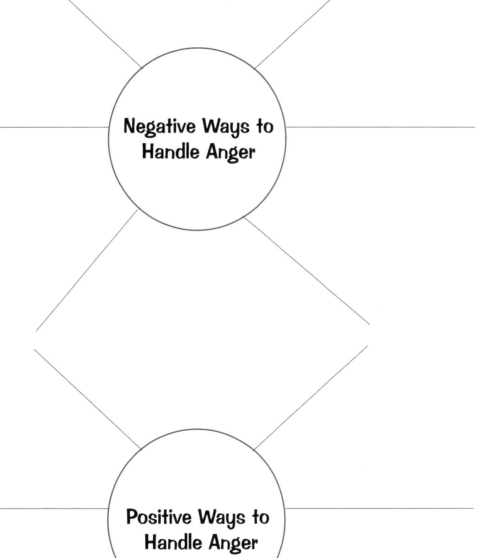

Negative Ways to Handle Anger

Positive Ways to Handle Anger

Objective: Students will recognize different types of bully behavior, become familiar with reasons for bullying, and learn ways to respond to bullies, both as victims and as bystanders.

Materials: "Anger's Way Out" by Karen Biron-Dekel, "Bully Questionnaire," pens.

Procedure:

<u>Part 1</u>

1. Read page 26 of "Anger's Way Out," in which students make fun of Sam's weight.

2. Explain that what happened to Sam is known as Bullying. Bullying is when someone intentionally hurts another person who is smaller or weaker, to make themselves feel powerful.

3. Have students fill out the "Bully Questionnaire."

4. Put the following headings on the board: Types of Bullying, Reasons for Bullying, Responses to Bullying: Victim/Bystander

5. Ask students to name types of Bullying, i.e., name calling, teasing, threatening, intimidating, fighting, cyber-bullying, or trying to force someone to do something they don't want to do. List and discuss. Add any they may have missed.

6. Next have students brainstorm reasons for Bullying, i.e., power, attention, poor self-esteem, learned behavior (they themselves were bullied), etc. List on board, adding any they might have missed, and discuss i.e., "Sometimes the only way someone knows how to feel good is by making someone else feel bad."

7. Discuss the role of the bystander and how they can influence bully behavior (i.e., by not encouraging the bully, not laughing, not being silent, telling someone, distracting, comforting the victim, etc). List these under Responses to Bullying along with suggestions for Victim Responses to Bullying.

Part 2

1. Students should complete the 1st page of the "What Would You Do?" Handout.

2. When they are finished, break them into small groups and instruct them to cooperatively answer the questions on the 2nd sheet. Designate one person in each group to write the responses on the handout of what the group decides is the best answer to each question.

3. Return to the larger group. Ask them which questions they found the hardest to answer. Discuss their responses.

Bully Questionnaire

Directions: Complete the questions below and share with the class or another student.

1. Has anyone ever made fun of you or bullied you?

   _____

   _____

2. What happened?

   _____

   _____

3. How did you feel inside?

   _____

   _____

4. How did you act? What did you say?

   _____

   _____

5. Are you happy with the way you handled the situation?

   _____

   _____

6. What could you do differently next time?

_____

_____

7. Have you ever witnessed someone else being made fun of?

_____

_____

8. What did you do?

_____

_____

9. Do you think you did the right thing?

_____

_____

10. What else could you have done?

_____

_____

What Would YOU Do???

a) The new girl in class, Emily, asked Sam for a play date. When Sam's friends found out, they told her that they don't like Emily. If Sam hangs out with her, they won't be friends with her anymore.

b) Kevin was riding his bike to practice, when he passed a few of the popular kids walking together. "Hey, Kevin, where did you get that bike, the Salvation Army?" Everyone started laughing.

c) Laquanda's best friend, Sarah, has been distancing herself since she started hanging out with a new group of girls from her soccer team. Today, as she walked to the lunch table, Sarah gave her a dirty look and started whispering to her new friends. They all looked at Laquanda and started giggling.

d) Tyrone was walking to school, when Matt, a big kid in his gym class, came up to him and asked for a dollar. Tyrone said, "No." Matt replied, "If you don't give me the money, I'll see you after school." Matt's friend yelled, "What's the matter, wus, you afraid to fight?"

Name the bully, victim, and bystander in each situation.

a)_____ _____ _____

b)_____ _____ _____

c)_____ _____ _____

d)_____ _____ _____

Describe the type of bully behavior in each scenario.

a)_____

b)_____

c)_____

d)_____

What do you think was the reason for the bully behavior in each scenario?

a)_____

b)_____

c)_____

d)_____

What would you have done if you were the victim in each scenario?

a)_____

b)_____

c)_____

d)_____

What would you have done if you were the bystander in each scenario?

a)_____

b)_____

c)_____

d)_____

About the Author

Karen Biron-Dekel is an author, counselor, and parent who is keenly aware of the many challenges that children face in today's society. Her goal is to help them identify their stressors and deal with them in a  constructive way. As a school counselor, Ms. Biron-Dekel works primarily with students at the middle school level. In addition, she has run divorce support groups for children, parenting groups for adults, and does presentations at conferences for mental health professionals. She received her B.A. in Psychology from Stony Brook University in New York, graduating Phi Beta Kappa, and holds a Master of Arts Degree in Counseling from Hofstra University, N.Y. Ms. Biron-Dekel has two grown children and lives in Oceanside, N.Y., with her husband.